ALLAN M LAYNE
I0771675
THE STRONTUM-9
AFFAIR

THE STRONTUM-9 AFFAIR

ALLAN M. LAYNE

Kravitz & Sons

Kravitz and Sons LLC
1301 Farmville Blvd, Suite 104
Greenville, NC 27834

Published by Kravitz and Sons LLC.

ISBN: 979-8-89639-018-3 (sc)
ISBN: 979-8-89639-017-6 (e)

Library of Congress Control Number: 2024924406

Table of Contents

All characters are fictitious except for the little girl lost, Captain John Sheeny, retired eastern airline pilot who helped me fly the A330 plane back to IAD.

Acknowledgments

Rachel Cartwright editor and literary design

It is Friday, March 6, and the weather has been cold. It's the kind of cold that seems to go through everything that you're wearing, so I take a few days off and stay home and finish the novel I'm reading by Stephen King. The weekend passed rather quickly and quietly. Naturally, I did spend some time at The Friendly Post to have a couple of beers.

Now I'm on my way to the office to file away my latest case, the kidnapping of Bumpy Jackson's daughter. See, Bumpy is a small-time pimp with a thriving business, pushing Blue Sky through his sanitation business. His daughter was snatched by a small group of boppers as she was leaving classes at Georgetown University, and they wanted to extort money out of him for her release.

Both father and daughter are united back home now, thanks to yours truly here, and Bedilia. Who is Bedilia, you ask? Well, she is my Berretta, and I keep her tucked nice and warm under my arm. She doesn't like it when I have to reach in and jerk her awake because she comes out chattering to beat the band. I can assure you, when she's done, she's chopped a few bodies into meat.

I hear on the radio there were four deadly explosions—one in the Soviet Union, and in China, Iran and North Africa. It seems to me that the terrorists are definitely planning to blow up the world.

It's 9:10 a.m. when I arrive at the office and hang up my coat and hat. I walk over to the file cabinet, take out a glass and a bottle of cognac, and pour out a three-fingers' size shot. As I sit down behind my desk, I see that my answering machine light is blinking. I reach to engage it, and a sudden chill grips me. A chill of fear. I take a deep sip of my drink and savor it, slowly. It is very warming. I lean back in my chair and listen to the message:

"Mr. Delaplane, my name is Allan Layne, president of Layne Industries, and I would like to meet with you around 4:00 p.m. My office is at 1608 Greenwich Way, Suite 608, and my number is 703-555-3838."

When the recording stops, I think, "why would a call like that cause me fear?" I take another sip from my drink and proceed to finish filing away the Bumpy Jackson case.

Around 3:00 p.m., I get into my car and head over to Greenwich Way. I arrived a little early, but I still take the elevator to the sixth floor. When I enter Mr. Layne's executive office, I'm met by the receptionist.

"Hi, my name is Jack Delaplane, and I'm here to see Mr. Layne."

"I'm Lynette Soyahn. I've heard of you," she says with a smile. "Your reputation precedes you. You're one of the five greatest detectives in Northern Virginia."

I reply, simply, "So they say."

She asks, "Have you met the other four, and who are they?"

"Yes, I have," I say, smiling again. "They are Jessie Stone, Sir James, Sidney Wong, and Sam Delaware."

She walks back to her desk and calls Mr. Layne to let him know that I'm here. All the while I can't help thinking how gorgeous she looks. As she escorts me in to see Layne, she writes something on a piece of paper, folds it, and stuffs it into my lapel pocket.

As she does so, her hand seems to trace the outline of Bedilia under my arm, and I can see the flash of excitement on her face. In that moment, I knew that I wanted to see more of Lynette Soyan. She opens the door, and I step into Layne's office. I turn to her and say, "I'll see you again?"

She flashes me a smile of reply. "Yes."

"Mr. Delaplane, I'm glad you came down on such short notice. Come on, sit down. Let me tell you why I called. Here at Layne Industries, we have been working on creating the ultimate atomic bomb using Strontum-9. Strontum-9 is a highly explosive element. We at Layne Industries have been able to stabilize it by using it in a crystallized form and, in this way, package and ship it to any destination without fear of detonation if it is dropped or mishandled.

"We instruct that the missile is delivered in the form of a 10,000-pound bomb along with liquid nitrogen. These two elements are mixed using a radio altimeter at 10,000-feet. The complete mixture is set to detonate at 500 above the ground, which is now an over-pressure bomb, or a conversion bomb.

"Our government is using this to get away from the "fireball" type of arsenal. This will wipe out the enemy within a two-mile radius.

"The world has been losing a lot of great scientists because Strontum-9 is too unstable. I am in the final stages of this project, but my notes of previous experiments are missing. I don't believe it's one of my employees because I designed the security signal grid, and no one else has access to it.

"Mr. Delaplane, I would like you to handle this case. If I call the police or the FBI, there stands a chance the evidence could get contaminated with all the handling procedures. I have set up an account of $200,000 which you can feel free to use for food, travel, lodging, whatever. My secretary will brief you on the account if you accept the case."

I can see that Mr. Layne is in a bit of a rush because he is pacing while talking and glancing at the time. The retainer was generous, and the excitement of such a case was something I couldn't turn down.

I shake hands with Mr. Layne to accept the case, and he escorts me back to his secretary's desk. My interest in his case has peaked with the mere thought of a destructive formula falling into the hands of a rogue country. Layne leaves the reception room and heads for the elevators. Before I leave, I turn to the receptionist.

"Miss Soyahn?"

She quickly stops me and says, "Lynette."

I smile again and say, "Okay. Lynette. Would you like to have dinner? I know a nice seafood restaurant in uptown Arlington called Xio [Shio] Lins."

She says, "I was hoping you would ask."

As we leave the building, she takes my hand, and we quicken our pace to the parking lot. She clicks the automatic door lock on her key ring and tosses me her keys. I bring the car engine to life, and off we go.

During dinner, we don't talk much about the case, except that she says she feels that her boss was very naïve in his thinking that an outsider is the source of his dilemma.

I asked her to explain.

"A man named Keattings has been with the firm for more than 15 years," she explains, "and money has not been a problem for him up to now, even after his wife divorced him. Now, he's barely making ends meet."

Lynette gave me a debit card to my new account, which I signed. Then she hands me a manila envelope and tells me to look it over when I have time.

As we sip from our wine glasses, she watches my eyes very closely.

Then, slowly, she asks, "Are you married?"

I tell her, "No," and proceed to explain the family-inherited illness that my wife had succumbed to. It is getting later, but the night is still young. We walked back to the car, and I opened the passenger door and let her in. As I slide in behind the wheel, she asks if I know my way to 10485 Fincastle Street.

I pulled into the driveway of Lynette's house, a nice size with a two-car garage and a neatly manicured lawn. We're at her door, and Lynette watches me analyze which key matches the lock. I open the door. She goes in and disarms the security alarm system. I follow her into the living room. She turns to me and says, "Make yourself at home, and I'll have the same drink that you're having."

I pull her close and kiss her. She kisses me back, long and reassuringly. We cross the living room to the sunroom where I mix two drinks of cognac and ginger ale.

We sip our drinks, and she clicks my glass in approval. "Cheers." We walk upstairs where she shows me the guest room where I can shower. She pulls me close and kisses me, smiles and says my name, "Jack Delaplane," then she turns and walks in the direction of another bedroom, which I presume is hers. As I showered, I lingered on the words she had uttered when we came in, "Make yourself at home." I dress and walk back downstairs, and she returns to meet me shortly, thereafter, appropriately wrapped in only a towel.

The next morning, I am awakened in a way that most guys only dream of. Afterwards, we shower, dress, and go downstairs for breakfast. It wasn't easy to pry myself away from Lynette, and I assured her that I would always look forward to more nights like that again with her.

I headed back to my place to look over the manila envelope she gave me. After I get home, I empty out the envelope contents on the table, pour myself another glass of cognac, and get down to business. The surveillance video was set up only for the last two weeks. The firm had something going on that was a distraction. The personnel folder on Keattings only covers the last two months. Here are three financial disclosures, and Lynette said her boss is very naïve in thinking that his problem is an outside source.

After a few minutes pondering the contents, I gasped out loud. "Lynette could be in danger!"

She put this packet together. If Keattings finds out that she suspects him, he just may put a contract out on her. He had access to Layne Industries assets, invested $7,000,000 in oil commodities when they were soaring and could make a bundle. Now that it has caved in on him, he's lost it all.

Frantically, I call Lynette. No answer. I'm thinking that by selling Layne's formula, Keattings could replace it all and say, "Sorry this all happened to you, boss." Now some rogue country has the superpower to do whatever it wants to the rest of the world. That's why Layne was in a hurry to get to New York and meet with the other members of the board of directors.

I jumped into the car and drove in a mad rush to Lynette's house. On the way, I called her again. This time she answers. I tell her to stay put and lock her doors, and I'll be there in 15 minutes to explain.

I pull into the driveway, screech to a stop, and run up the walkway. She quickly lets me in. We sit in the sunroom, and I tell her what I found out from the folder that she gave me and what Keattings might be planning. When I ask why her boss was in a hurry to get to New York, she confirms it: to meet with the board of directors.

I ask her to go pack some clothes, but before I can finish speaking, a burst of automatic gunfire smashes through the window. I push her to the floor and grab Bedilia, and she comes out chattering. Another automatic burst comes through the kitchen window, and Bedilia takes him down. Two shots now come from the living room but miss their mark. I put Lynette behind me to make our way to the dining room. That thug capped off two more rounds, and Bedilia answered. I feel the hot heat slam into my chest, and I slump to the floor. Another thug comes around the corner; before he can squeeze the trigger, Lynette grabs Bedilia and caps him between the eyes. Afterwards, she tapes me up with thick gauze to stem the blood flow.

"Let's get out of here before the cops arrive. I'll explain to them later, after I close this case out," I say.

She wants to take me to a hospital, but I say, "No. Take me to the No- name Bar in the village."

On the way, I telephone Bumpy Jackson to meet me there with his doctor and two of his men. I ask Lynette, "How did you learn to shoot like that?"

She replies, "It's just instinct. I emulated you, and I didn't want to lose you."

"It's almost 7:30 p.m.," I say. "You better call your boss in New York, and let him know you're okay. Tell him to stay there a couple of days. With this all over the news, no telling who Keattings will try to take out now that he's flushed out in the open."

Xio Chen is working the bar. I tell her to let us into the back room and also to let in Bumpy and his men in when they arrive. After a few minutes, Bumpy comes in.

"Delaplane, are you okay? Something big must be going down."

"Yeah, I need your Doc to get this slug out of me and patch me up pretty tight because I have to make my move right away."

Bumpy asks, "Do you have a plan?"

"Don't give me a shot for the pain, Doc; it will just numb me all over. Ask Xio Chen to send me a shot of something, and you guys can get what you want."

I turn to Lynette and tell her I am the owner of the No-name Bar.

"I have a gut feeling that Keattings may try to get out of the country and make a quick sale to recoup his financial losses. And he just may try to find another county to reside in. If that's the case, can any of you gentlemen travel with me out of the country to help me with this case?"

Before they can answer, the doctor starts working on me. After a few painful minutes of probing, the doctor finally gets the slug out and wraps me up pretty tight. I look at him and say, "Being painless is not your specialty, is it, Doc?"

He looks at me and replies, "I didn't feel a thing."

Everyone laughs. Bumpy says, "If it's out of the country, we won't be able to help you, Jack."

I turn to Lynette and say, "I want you to go to my place, 1501 Union Avenue. Stay there while I close this out."

She says, "No, John, I want to be with you. Call the police. Let them handle it from here."

"No, it's not that simple. If they close the case, this formula is put in their holding bin. What if someone takes it from there? We're back to square one. Here are my keys. Also, I need you to see if Keattings has booked a flight overseas. If he did, call me right away."

Thirty minutes later, Lynette calls me back to tell me that Keattings has booked a 9:20 p.m. flight out of Dulles to Shanghai.

I think, "So much for planning…" I then asked her to check my phone directory and call Inspector Sidney Wong to see if he can help me. If he can, I tell her to go ahead and brief him, and I will be in Shanghai Airport in 11 hours and 45 minutes. I will be flying my own plane out of Manassas Airport.

I asked Bumpy to drop me off at the airport, thanking all for being ready to help me out.

Jung Lee is just coming in to work at the Manassas Airport; I ask her if she'll help me with the flight to Shanghai. Naturally, she says, "Yes," because now she has a free trip back to see her parents. Miss Lee had flown as my flight steward when some corporate bigwigs leased my private plane. She has also helped me with flying over the past five years, so she knows my plane well. We will be going east over Ireland, which should take five refueling stops; that would take a lot out of me if I did it alone.

When we arrived in Shanghai, it's late, and I have lost a whole day because of the International Date Line change. We can use the rest, though, and the time to research where Keattings may go to sell the formula. I park the plane, and Inspector Wong meets me inside the hangar. Over the next few hours of phone calls, Inspector Wong learns that Keattings has a meeting set up at Lee Ki Industry. Wong has some friends on the inside; I tell him to have his friends divert the meeting to a less crowded part of the building where he and I will be waiting to greet him. Now I can get some much-needed rest.

When we arrive at Lee Ki Industry, Inspector Wong checks with his inside contacts to see when and where Keattings will be meeting to make his sale. We are told that the meeting has been cancelled. That is not good news. This is now turning into one of those "needle in the haystack" jobs.

Inspector Wong asks, "Now what do we do?"

I reply, "I don't think China was offering him as much as he wanted. I'm sure he's looking elsewhere in a panic, and now our job has gotten tougher. Let's go to your office."

On the way to Wong's office, my mind is racing to figure out Keattings's next move. It's now 9:30 a.m. Working a job like this in China is not the same as we do it back in the States. We have surmised that for Keattings to go to the Soviet Union to cut a deal is out. My guess is that he will try Iran first over North Africa because that is a wealthy country. Wong starts making a few calls to his connections in

Interpol. It's now 10:45 a.m.; we learn that my guess is right. Keattings has booked a 5:30 p.m. flight to Tehran.

Now I am lost as to where to start looking for a contact that he may have there. I make a call back to the States to Layne Industries. It's still daylight there.

Lynette answers the phone, and I ask her to check her boss's files for an address in Iran that was doing some tests on Strontum-9 and to call me back at Wong's number, which I give her. I don't want to tell her too much over the phone for several reasons. One, it wasn't going to make our job any easier by telling her everything, and, two, because of the open phone lines. It takes her some time to call back, and she gives me Shah Industry. Now, the problem is how to put a plant there since we know nothing about the firm and no one by name that's working there.

"Well, Wong, I think we should show up at the airport around 3:30 p.m. to actually see Keattings get on the flight. Then we will take my plane to Iran and try to figure out a way to capture him there. What do you think?"

"Your plan sounds good so far."

"Drop me off at the hotel, Mr. Wong, so I can get some rest. And you'd better get some rest, too, so that you can help me with the flying."

Later that afternoon, Wong picks me up, and we stake out the airport for Keattings's arrival. Sure enough, we spot him walking towards the Iran Air ticket counter. I recognize him from his photo in the manila envelope Lynette gave me. We follow at a safe distance behind him as he goes through the security screening. We exit the terminal and go to where I've parked my plane. I call the tower to file a regular flight plan to dispel any notions of secrecy for which we can be detained or delayed for a long period of time. We are off the ground at 4:30 p.m.

When we arrive in Iran, I convert $5,000 to their currency and brief Mr. Wong on my plan. All plans are made on short notice. Wong agrees; it's feasible.

"What we need to do, Wong, is stop him before he gets into the meeting to sell the documents."

Wong says, "You are right. If we get into a shooting match and kill some Iranians, we will not get out alive, and they will get the documents anyway."

"If something happens to one of us," I say, "the other one will have to get out of the country with the documents and return them to Layne Industries. Let's go and locate Shah Industry and find the meeting place."

We drive to Shah Industry, which is located to the south and east of the capital city of Tehran for about an hour and 15 minutes, just to nose around and see if we can get an advantage. Many years ago, this was a very nice place to come to for your vacation. My favorite place has always been the ancient capital of Isfahan. We walked to the guard shack, and I greeted the guard in his own language. His name is Anoush, and he speaks very good English to us, seeing that I am an American and Wong is Chinese. After a lengthy talk and an exchange of a tidy sum of money, he tells us everything we want to know, right down to which building the meeting will take place in with Keattings—tomorrow at 9:00 a.m.—and that he will be working that morning. Now, everything is falling into place.

The next morning, we arrive early, at 8:35 a.m., and Anoush, the guard, is there as promised. We go in and position ourselves to get an advantage on Keattings before he can get to the meeting room. We put silencers on our guns to muffle our shots, if any.

A limo drives up, and a stocky middle-aged man gets out and walks toward the entrance. It's Keattings. He goes into the building and makes his way towards the back office. I called out to get his attention.

"Keattings, this is Inspector Delaplane, and you're under arrest for transporting stolen documents for illegal sales."

Slowly, he turns towards me. I'm out in the open. He quickly jumps behind a desk, grabs his gun, and shoots. His shot hits me just above the heart. I return fire as does Inspector Wong. Wong grabs the briefcase and checks him over. He's dead.

Wong tries to help me up, but I tell him I can't make it. He pulls me up anyway. We make it back to the car and start the slow and fast drive back to the airport in a controlled way so as not to arouse any suspicion. We quickly board my plane, and Wong rummages through the medicine kit to find something to patch me up.

Wong says, "Hang in there, buddy; I'll get us out of here. I know the Shanghai Airport approaches; they have the best doctors. We're going to Shanghai!"

Wong files a flight plan to get us back to Shanghai. The trip is long—seven hours and 10 minutes, and I keep waking and passing out. Just before we touch down, Wong tells the tower to have an ambulance standing by for an injured passenger. When we touched down, the ambulance was there, and I am rushed immediately to a Shanghai hospital. After waiting for almost an hour and not hearing anything on my condition, Inspector Wong boards a late flight to Washington Dulles Airport.

The next afternoon, Inspector Wong pays a visit to Layne Industries. He is met by the receptionist.

"Good afternoon. I am Inspector Wong, and I would like to see Mr. Allan Layne."

During the introduction, a tall gentleman enters the room. "I'm Allan Layne."

Wong says, "Let me see some identification because I've lost a very good friend recovering this, and I don't want to be giving it up to the wrong person."

Layne produces a driver's license.

Inspector Wong gives him the briefcase, which he opens and confirms it's the Strontum formula. Lynette questions him as to what happened to Jack Delaplane because this was his case.

Wong explains to her that he was shot, and he doesn't know if he survived. Lynette sinks into her chair. She is very hurt and heartbroken. She weeps silently. After a few minutes, she tells her boss that she wants to go home; she isn't feeling well and needs the next day off also. Layne lets her leave.

The following week, Marisa from finance rushes upstairs to see Mr. Layne. She asks him about a bill she's received from Shanghai's hospital, which she paid, but now she's got another one. She wants to know who is assigned there.

Lynette, listening to this, puts it all together. Delaplane is still alive. She tells her boss that she wants to go on vacation, effective now. She takes the bill from Marisa and says, going out the door, "I'll take care of this."

On the way home to pack, she calls to book a 10:30 a.m. flight to Shanghai. She arrives late the next day and takes a taxi to Shanghai's hospital. She inquires at the information desk: "Which room is Jack Delaplane's?"

Her heartbeat has quickened now. She hurriedly takes the elevator to the third floor and quickly walks to room 315. She opens the door. There he is. With a happy smile on her face, she embraces him.

"John."

They embrace as if they want to be joined as one, and Delaplane answers her, "Lynette."

After a few minutes, she tells him that she's brought him some clothes and to get dressed. "Let's go home."

As they are leaving the hospital room, he says, "I almost forgot." He crosses the room, picks up his other blazer, reaches into the lapel pocket, and takes out a folded sheet of paper. He also puts his old clothes into a bag and takes them with him. Walking down the hallway, he unfolds the paper and reads: "Call me." I most certainly will do that.

I wasn't strong enough to make the flight back just yet. I called Jung Lee's parents' house to see if she was still there. I got lucky; she said that she would stay another three days as long as I paid her salary.

A few days later, we've arrived, back in Virginia. The next business day, I go to Layne Industries to Layne's office to confirm he has received all of his documents. Of course, my main reason for going there is to see Lynette again and tell her that I love her.

Mr. Layne flew to New York to meet with his board of directors and let them know how close the world had come to being destroyed. He sternly emphasized that Strontum-9 is just too unstable, that testing should cease by all countries, and that they should stick to peaceful negotiations for a resolution.

●●●

Here it is, April 3, and it has been a fast-paced month. I've halfway finished filing away the Strontum-9 case when a thought comes to me. That chill of fear that gripped me initially could have been that chill of death that seems to follow me on every case. My phone rings, and I answer it.

"Inspector Delaplane."

Lynette says, "Hi, I'm on my way to pick you up. Let's go to the No-name Bar. It's Friday, and I want to see if I can like it."

It's 3:30 p.m. when Lynette arrives at my office. While I'm putting things away, my door opens and in walks a little girl of maybe 11 years old.

"Are you Mr. Delaplane?"

"Yes, I am. What can I do for you?"

"I would like for you to help me find my sister."

Lynette walks over to her, gives her a hug, looks at me, looks back at her, and says, "Yes, we will help you find her. Did you get separated while shopping in a store?"

"No, she was taken from the hospital two days ago."

"The missing Davidson Girl."

The T.V. news flash comes rushing back to me as I slump back into my chair.

"John, I'm sorry," says Lynette.

"I didn't know."

"That's okay," I tell her.

"I'll take care of it."

Years ago, when I started in this business as a young, hungry, and anxious P.I., I would take on every job that came my way—divorce cases, murder cases, runaways, insurance fraud cases… I have done them all. I never liked the divorce cases. Even today, I try to avoid them because of the pain and trauma the whole family has to suffer. Now, I relish the insurance fraud and murder cases; however, this one that just walked into my office will require a lot of luck.

It will be like looking for a needle in a haystack. I have a two-day head start. Otherwise, I could be running halfway around the world chasing leads that will turn into false leads. But be that as it may, I have already looked into her big brown eyes, and I can't say no to finding a little girl lost.

The room falls silent for a short moment as the little girl reaches into a shopping bag that she's carrying. She pulls out a piggy bank, puts it on my desk, and pushes it towards me, saying, "I have lots of money to pay you."

I exhale, lean onto my desk, and ask, "Ms. Davidson, what is your first name?"

"Maryann," the little girl answers.

"Okay, Maryann. I want you to call your mom for me." I gave her the phone. She dials the number, then hands the phone back to me.

"Hello, Mrs. Davidson? This is Jack Delaplane, and I have your daughter, Maryann, in my office. Can you come down to my office?"

She says yes, and that she's on her way. After reading the little girl's face and eyes, I couldn't find one reason to say no to taking her case.

Twenty minutes pass, and her mother enters my office with tears welling in her eyes because I'm sure she thought she'd lost a second daughter. She apologizes over and over for her daughter coming to my office, and I assure her that she hasn't inconvenienced me.

My question to her now is how her daughter heard of me. Maryann speaks up. She says she heard her dad telling her mom how great I am and that it costs a lot of money to hire me. I tell her that I will take on this job with a very high priority and that my fee for her daughter is a one-dollar bill. Maryann gives me a big smile and a big hug. She reaches into her little purse and gives me a fairly crisp one-dollar bill. I escort mother and daughter to the door, and they say goodbye again with heartfelt thanks and leave.

I walk back to my desk, pick up my car keys, and Lynette and I are headed out the door. I stop at her car and tell her I want to cancel our date for tonight because of my urgency to get what I can about the missing Davidson girl. She says that she understands and apologizes for volunteering me without fully understanding what is going on.

I drove down to police headquarters to talk with my friend, Lt. Vic Gallini. I decided to use the social approach with him and let him spill the beans about this case.

When I enter Gallini's office, his first words are, "Delaplane! Am I glad to see you!"

"Well, I'm just dropping by to see what's going on with you."

"I guess you heard about the baby getting snatched from the hospital yesterday?"

"Yes, I have."

"Well, we have gone over that security tape with a fine-tooth comb and can't find anything."

"Vic, well, if you want, I'll look it over, and who knows? Fresh eyes may come up with something. May I have a copy of the tape?"

"Sure, take this one; we have made extras."

I return to my office with the tape to review it. It's Friday night. I've canceled my date, so my calendar for tonight is open. Besides, I would like to find out as much as I can while the case is still fresh.

Lt. Gallini said he checked the tape with a fine-tooth comb and couldn't find anything, so I guess I better start looking for the not-so-obvious. While viewing the tape, a lady's face shows up on the window of the hospital nursery, but the tape is too grainy. She has blonde hair, which I'm sure is a wig. Two hours have gone by and, nothing.

Finally, "Ah." I stop the tape and do a short, slow playback. I stop the tape again and scan the picture. That long look shows that the woman has a deformity. She has an elevated right shoe. Her right hand, there's something wrong; she can't open it fully. Well, now, Vic, old buddy, you just may have given me something to go on.

From the tape, she looks to be about 5' 6", 135 pounds, maybe Caucasian, and about 37 years old. I feel that I'm at a point now where I can stop for the night and get a fresh start tomorrow morning.

As I'm shutting everything down and reaching for my coat to leave, my phone rings. I look at my watch. 11:45 p.m.

"Jack Delaplane."

"Delaplane, this is Inspector Wong. How are you?" "I'm doing fine, thanks."

"That's good. The reason I called is to let you know that Strontum-9 is starting to show its face again."

"Mr. Wong, Layne Industries said that it would push the UN to shut down all Strontum-9 experiments."

"Well, Jack, you know there are some rogue countries out there that will stop at nothing to gain a little power."

"Let me get back to you. Right now, I'm on a case where I have very few clues and very little time to act."

"Good night, Delaplane."

After we hang up, I head out the door with another question on my mind which I'll address later.

It's almost 9:30 a.m. Saturday morning when I arrive at the DMV keeping my fingers crossed that they will be willing to work with me without a lot of red tape. I proceed to the information desk and ask if I can speak with the on-duty supervisor. No sooner do I sit down and pull out my notes, when a young lady approaches me.

"Hi, my name is Ms. Weston."

"Hi, my name is Jack Delaplane. Can we talk—in your office?" "Sure, right this way."

As she's closing the door to her office behind us, I ask her, "Have you heard about the kidnapping from the hospital nursery?" I show her my shield and license and tell her that I'm a P.I. working on the case.

"Yes, I have, and that is so sad. The police are confounded with no information. They seem to be at a standstill."

I tell her, "You've very observant; however, I believe that person is still here in the city and in your database."

"You have my utmost support. What can I do for you?"

"If you can do a search on applicants applying for handicap tags, that is where I would like to start."

"Yes, I can do that, but that will produce a lot of people."

"Okay, how about if we narrow it down to just females?" She says, "Okay, that's better."

"Well, let me give you a shorter search, hopefully."

"Let's do: females, Caucasian, 37 years of age, about 5'6", and 135 pounds."

She says, "This is a good search, and it's not going to produce a long list for you."

"Thank you very much for your help, Ms. Weston."

"I don't know how long it will take, but here is my card."

"I will work this case 24 hours a day if I have to. Call me any time." She says, "This case must mean a lot to you, then?"

"It does. The baby's 11-year-old sister is my client. She came to my office to ask me to help her find her sister. When I looked into her little lost face and eyes, I just couldn't refuse. I thought they were separated while shopping, but when she told me the story, my heart went out to her. You know, Ms. Weston, no client has ever given me everything they have to take a case. Well, she offered me her piggy bank."

"Mr. Delaplane, you are a very special and caring person to take on this case from your heart. I will get this to you as soon as I can."

We shared small talk as she escorted me all the way out to the building exit. It was as if she didn't want our chance meeting to end so soon. Any other time I would have followed through on that notion, but time is not on my side with this case.

I bid Ms. Weston goodbye, hopped into my car, and headed uptown. I keep waiting to pat myself on the back for what I've accomplished, but a voice in my head keeps telling me, not yet.

I hit the speed-dial on my car phone and call Inspector Jessie Stone. After two rings, she picks up. "This is Jessie Stone."

"How are you doing Inspector? This is Delaplane."

"Jack Delaplane, my goodness, I thought you were dead. Wong called me two weeks ago and said you got shot on a job in Shanghai with him. How are you?"

"I'm doing fine. They have to put more than two holes in me to stop me. I really need your help, Jessie. I'm almost between a rock and a hard place."

"I'll will be glad to help you, Jack. Where are you?"

"I'm on my way uptown. Can you meet me at the No-name Bar?"

"Of course, I will be there in 30 minutes."

Now I can say that I'm starting to feel a little better. Fifteen minutes later, I pulled into the reserve parking space of the big-hearted owner of the No-name Bar. I walk in, and I'm greeted by Xio Chen. I say to her, "What's a good-looking lady like you doing in a place like this?"

"You hired me," she says, "and this is the best club in town. Boss, you should buy the space next door and expand. You have more than enough clientele to support an expansion."

"Xio, why don't you do that? Design the expansion; get a builder. I don't want you to leave and work someplace else."

She slides a glass of cognac on the rocks in front of me.

"Xio Chen, when you get the ball rolling on this project, and I know it's going be a lot of work, you can give yourself a raise. When it's almost finished, you can start hiring more staff."

Just then, Inspector Jessie Stone comes in, walks over to the bar. I introduce the two ladies.

"Xio Chen, this is Inspector Stone; Inspector, Xio Chen." I asked Xio to fix her a gin martini with three olives.

"So this is your place... Wow. You should expand it." Xio Chen interjects, "We were just talking about that." We excuse ourselves and move to a booth to talk.

"Jess, I'm glad you came down on such a short request." I tell Jess the story of my latest assignment, all the way down to my search on the DMV files. I explain also my need for a female on the case with me because some places are off-limits to men.

"Jack, I've always known you to have a big heart. For you to take this job on for free, I'll help you. I've made enough to satisfy both my needs and my caprices. And from the looks of your club, I can say the same for you."

Just then my phone rings. "Jack Delaplane."

"Hi, Mr. Delaplane, this is Sharon Weston. I have the list that you requested."

"That's great. Right now, I'm in discussion with my partner on the case."

"Where do you live?" "I live in Ashland."

"So do I. Can you take it home with you, and I'll swing by later and pick it up?"

"I'll bring it to your place; what's your address?"

"1501 Union Avenue."

I topped off our meeting by telling Jess how Lt. Gallini couldn't find anything on the tape, so he gave it to me. As we're getting up to leave, I leave a $20 on the table for the waitress and say goodnight to Xio Chen.

I can see Jess is parked next to my car. As she presses the remote unlock on her key ring and gets into her car, I tell her that I'm starting to feel better about our chances of finding the infant.

Before I get into my car, I called Ms. Weston back to see what time she can be at my place. She tells me 9:00 p.m.

I still have some time to kill, so I go back inside. Xio Chen fixes me another drink, and I go into the back office and call Vic. He tells me that they still have nothing to go on. They had dusted for prints, but being a hospital, everything was clean.

I don't tell Gallini what I've come up with. His captain would want to take over the investigation, and as usual, they would blow it. He stops me short of hanging up and says, "Delaplane, come over to my office; I need to see you. It's urgent."

"I'm on my way."

As I'm leaving, I ask Xio Chen if she's serious about expanding the No- name Bar. Her answer is a resounding yes. On my way out, I say to her, "Don't break the bank."

She blows me a kiss, and I say, "See you later."

I needed that invite to stop in and see Vic. He may have had something else to pass on to me. When I walk in, he assures me that nothing got leaked to the press. At that point, I want to tell him about the hunch I have and what I'm working on, but I don't. He also tells me that no ransom has been demanded for the return of the infant. That solidifies my hunch that my suspect is too old to have one of her own, plus being handicapped, she wanted a healthy baby.

I finally get back home and pull into my driveway, and a car pulls in beside me. I can see that it's Sharon.

"Hi, John. Can I call you 'John'?"

"You sure can, come on in." I take the folder from her, and we walk inside the house. I escort her to the sunroom and drop the folder on my desk.

"You have yourself a beautiful house; it's so big. You live by yourself?"
"Yes, my wife died about eight years ago."

"I'm not married, either."

"So, Sharon, would you like to have a drink?" "Sure, whatever you're having."

As I'm fixing the drinks, I commence to apologize for taking up so much of her time.

"Sharon, the information that I've shared with you is just a hunch. I haven't told the police about it, so I need you to stay silent about it."

"Trust me, I will."

I can see from her eyes that she is taking in everything about my place, so I give her a quick tour, pointing out that the basement and deck are places where I like hanging out. We stand out on the deck, observing the dense fog that has now settled on the community.

The next morning, I get up around 6:30 a.m. and get dressed. I leave Ms. Weston a note saying that I want to start my surveillance of the names on the printed list.

I buy a breakfast sandwich and a coffee at Mac's and proceed to the first address on the list. After seeing the family coming out of the house, I quickly dismiss them as well as the next dozen names. They just don't fit what I'm looking for. My cell phone rings.

"Delaplane."

"Hi, it's Jessie. Can you meet me at the coffeehouse near your place?" "I'm on my way."

When I arrive, Jess is already there. She has a carafe on the table, so I sit down with her. I take out the folder and show her the list.

"Jack, your thinking is always ahead of everyone else's. This is great. Now, I told you I would help you with this case, so don't even think about having all the fun by yourself. Give me half of that list."

I give her half the names, and we set out to do surveillance. We drive back and forth, throughout the county roads—a very large area—and cross off addresses. We simply aren't getting a match on what we're looking for.

Anyone else would have said it was a wasted day and effort. But that's the nature of the business. Me, I looked at it as a very productive day because it eliminated what I didn't want right away. It's almost 8:30 p.m. when I tell Jess to meet me back at the No-name Bar.

When I get there, Xio Chen is working the bar, looking gorgeous as ever. I tell her Inspector Stone and I have finished our work for the day. Just then, Jess walks in.

Xio Chen fixes us each a drink, and we go into the back office. After about 45 minutes, we establish our game plan for tomorrow. She also feels that it was a productive day for us, and she, too, feels positive that, within 48 hours, we will close this case. I walked Jess out to her car and thank her again for her help on this case.

I go back into the office to get my folder, and as I am leaving, I say to Xio Chen, "What's a gorgeous lady like you doing in a place like this?"

"Waiting for you to ask me out."

That really puts a big smile on my face, so I say to her, "Tell Auhn Lee to close up tonight so that you can leave."

"Do you mean that? I've waited a long time for you to take me out."

"Yes, I mean it. I'll leave my car here, and we'll go in yours."

The drive to Xio Chen's place is enlightening and amusing. She wants to know if she has to call me "Boss." I laugh and tell her to call me John and that "Jack" is short for John.

A short while, later we pull into the driveway to her house, a very big house with a two-car garage located in The Brittney Community. We go in, and she silences her alarm system. She takes her shoes off near the door, and I reach down and take off mine. I slip my arms around her and hug her close, and we share a kiss. After a few more short kisses, I let her slip off my coat, and she loosens my tie.

Now I am starting to see the real beauty of Xio Chen. We go into the sunroom, and she mixes two drinks. She looks up at me and says, "I've started liking the same drink." She sips her drink, then puts it on the coffee table, kisses me, and says my name: "Jack Delaplane."

Then she goes upstairs, a short while later returning and wearing a Chinese lounge outfit that is thinner than smoke. She is absolutely beautiful. I kiss her again and tell her so.

We both awake the next morning about 7:00 a.m., and after toast and coffee, I tell her about my appointment with Jess Stone. "Okay, I'll drop you off at your car," she says, and she kisses me close. She drops me off, and I proceed to the coffee shop. A short while later, Jess and I are crossing off addresses again.

No sooner than Jess and I split up to start our surveillance of suspects, my phone rings again.

"Jack Delaplane."

"Yes, sir. This is Dr. Bakersfield. I'm at my clinic, the address is 107 Main Street. I'm having trouble here…diagnosing a patient."

The call is perplexing to me, but without hesitation, I answer swiftly, "I'm on my way."

Right away, I speed-dial Jess.

"Hi, Jess. Drop what you're doing and meet me at 107 Main Street. I just got a strange call from the clinic there from the doctor, and his voice sounded guarded. I don't think he was in a position to talk freely."

Inside of 10 minutes, we arrive, and I tell the receptionist to give us two lab coats.

Disguised as lab technicians, we go in and find a baby on the table being cared for by a nurse. There is another person in the room—a lady is standing about three feet away.

I ask, "Dr. Bakersfield, what seems to be the problem?"

While he's talking, I notice the woman's right hand. Then I look down, and I see she's wearing an elevator boot. I glance at the doctor's chart, then turn to the lady and tell her, by name, "Ms. Wright, my name is Inspector Delaplane, and you're under arrest for the abduction of this infant."

She slumps down in the nearby chair and starts to cry.

"Jess, call Vic. Tell him to send a squad car over right away." I immediately call the Davidson family.

"Jack Delaplane here. I think we've found your infant daughter. Can you come down to the hospital immediately to the pediatrics floor?"

They were on the way. I asked the doctor if his nurse can help us take the baby from his office to the hospital.

"Yes."

At this time, the police arrived. I tell them to read the woman her rights and to book her. I called Vic back to tell him what went on and to meet us at the hospital right away.

Inside of 20 minutes, we're at the hospital. The Davidson family joins us about a minute later; so does Vic. I asked the doctor to make an ID from the footprint. He does, and it matches the "little girl lost."

Maryann runs in and runs up to me. She looks very happy. She gives me a hug and says, "Thank you, Mr. Delaplane, for helping me find my sister."

Jess comes over, and now Maryann gives Jess a hug. Jess looks into her eyes and face, then turns to me and says, "Now I see why you couldn't say, No."

•••

The next morning, I go to the office to close my files on the "little girl lost."

When I am halfway finished, I think about how luck played a big role in this the case. The baby had Rosella, nothing serious. And Dr. Bakersfield knew that if he called the police, they would be asking him a lot of questions as to why he called them, and with the lady right there, she would get spooked and run out. He knew that if he called me, I would play along and come right over out of curiosity. If that hadn't happened, I guess Jess and I would still be out crossing off addresses and going to the DMV with a different search criteria.

I finished filing the case. I call Jess to tell her that I'm taking an extended vacation, and I want her to take over, take all of my calls and my work—whatever cases that may come in, if she's interested. She says she'll handle it. Before I leave, I switch my phone over to her number.

Now, I am on my way to see my old buddy, Vic, to close out my report with him. Before I get there, though, I stop at a jewelry store to have them design a very stunning engagement ring.

Xio Chen has always been very special to me, and now is the right time to show it. I hang out with Vic for about two hours, then tell him I have to check on the renovations of my bar and that, as of today, I'm on extended vacation. "Please don't call me about taking any cases."

I arrive at the No-name Bar shortly after noon, and there is Xio Chen. She looks good wearing jeans and lady work boots. I walk over to her and give her a kiss, and we chat.

She tells me that the builders should be finished in three months. I ask her, "Xio, have you thought of a name for the bar, yet?"

"Yes, I have been thinking," she answers.

I say to her, "Come on, Xio. Let's go inside. They don't need us out here."

After a few hours going over her plans for the new bar and new employees, my phone rings. It's the jeweler to tell me that my gift is ready. I bring Xio with me under the guise that my watch is not working right. I present the ring to her right there in the store, and it makes me feel great.

I'm off from work for the next three weeks and thoroughly enjoying my new life. One evening after dinner with Xio, my phone rings.

"Hello?"

"Inspector Delaplane, this is Inspector Wong, how are you?" "I'm doing fine."

"Good, I need your help."

"Is it what we spoke of earlier?'

"Yes, sir, it is. Jack, we can't get any help on this from Interpol, MI5—or anyone. There's too much red tape. I called Inspector Stone, but I couldn't tell her much over the phone. She said she would help.

"Are you in?"

"Yes, sir, I am."

"That's good because she's has already booked a flight for tomorrow for both of you."

I hang up and call Jess. She confirms everything and agrees to pick me up tomorrow. I break the news to Xio Chen, and she tells me that it comes with the job. She's such a beautiful lady.

"Hello, this is Layne Industries; how can I help you?"

"This is Jack Delaplane, and I need a short meeting with Mr. Layne right away."

"Can you be here before 3:30?" "I'm on my way."

I arrived there after a 45-minute drive and took the elevator to the sixth floor. A new receptionist greeted me and escorted me into Laynes office, and I gave it no further thought.

"Mr. Layne, as you've probably heard Strontum-9 has resurfaced again. Inspector Wong called me today asking if I would help him with this case."

"I'll help you in any way that I can."

"If we can create a strong distrust between China and Iran, we can eliminate this problem."

While I was explaining my plan to him, he had one of his scientist bring in two vials for me which he explained their usages. I thanked him for his help and left.

Friday morning, Jess and I arrived in Shanghai. Wong picks us up and takes us to his office. We have to come up with a game plan. Wong suggests that we should go in under the cover of darkness, plant a few charges, and level the place. Jess's idea isn't any better.

Silence falls over the room as I continue to go over Wong's evidence material. I spell out to everyone what's going on. China has bankrolled the United States for a long time with a lot of money. Iran is rich enough to pay China a lot of money for its help in perfecting Strontum-9. I don't like either of their plans because it would cost too many lives. We have to end this research with Strontum-9—forever.

"According to your background research, this professor likes to eat dinner at the kebab restaurant on Main Street. What we'll do is induce mental fatigue in the professor by administering Trimeserall. The Chinese will think that Iran is torturing him, overworking him. They will then demand that he is brought back to China, and they will never send anyone there again.

"Jess, I want you to meet up with the professor there and give him the first dose. Wong will be there with you as Dr. Wong. On the second day, meet with him again, and give him the rest. The next day, when he goes to work, he will be too exhausted to get anything done. They will take him home to rest, and we'll snatch him from there. Here, Jess, here's his photo."

"Wong, I need you to rent us a Lear 60. All three of us are qualified to fly that make and model. Here are the two doses of Trimeserall, Jess. I got them from Layne Industries."

"You think of everything, Jack."

"I try, but Layne is the genius behind this. Just a few more things to cover, and we're finished for today. Wong, when they bring him back on the third day, we will follow them."

"Once you're inside the house, inject the professor with this. It will slowly counteract his stupor. When everyone leaves, we'll rush the professor to our jet and get out of there."

Wong says, "I hope it goes as smoothly as this plan. I'm sure the driver will go back and tell his boss about you, so we'll have to move quickly."

"When we get to the airport, Jess will start the engines with a flight plan clearance of VFR on top Fl 180 to Russia. Now, it's Friday night, and there's nothing more to go over—unless there's something you two wish to discuss?"

"No."

"No."

"We are your guests in your country, Inspector Wong. By the way, I'm hungry."

The time has passed rather quickly, and now it's Sunday afternoon, and we're on our way to the uncertainty that lies ahead.

It's 6:30 p.m. when we land in Tehran. We checked into the hotel. Afterwards, we decide to recon Shah Industry, the kebab restaurant and the professor's house. The restaurant is very accessible as is his house, with no guards posted. From there to the airport back downtown is doable.

"Now, since there are no more questions, jump-off time is 7:00 a.m. Let's get some sleep."

The next morning, we all get into the limo to stake out the professor's house to see what time he leaves. Plus, this gives Jess a look, up close, at him.

Just as we get there, a car pulls up, and the professor comes out of the house and gets in. We go to the end of the street, turn around, and follow, but not too close. The trip is roughly 30 minutes to Shah Industry.

"Okay, Jess, you got a good look at the professor—you and Wong will be dinning with him tonight."

"Yes."

"Let's go to the airport to make sure the plane is fueled."

We spend the rest of the day just passing time. At 3:30 p.m., we arrive back at Shah Industry to wait for the professor to leave.

"Remember," I say," if the professor starts to get edgy or suspicious, break off the meeting, and excuse yourselves and leave. We will try to come up with a different plan." It turns out to be a short wait. Right at 4:00 p.m., he comes out and gets into the same waiting vehicle.

The streets are very crowded with cars and bicycles, and with people crossing anywhere and everywhere with no regard to the traffic.

Twenty minutes later, he pulls up to the restaurant and goes inside, and his driver leaves. We pull up; Jess and Wong go inside, and I park the car and enter the restaurant, too.

I sit at a vantage point across the room where the professor can't see my activity.

Wong makes the introductions.

"Good afternoon sir. I am Dr. Wong and this is my lab assistant, Ms. Jessie Stone."

"Good afternoon, I am Professor Sun. I am pleased to meet you. Please sit down."

They all sit down, and 25 minutes into the meeting, Wong distracts the professor by writing something on a napkin. While leaning over to see it, Jess administers the first vial in his drink. As the dinner is winding down, Wong insists that he will pick up the tab.

"Professor Sun, I have enjoyed having dinner with you. Let me take care of the check."

This is a very good move. He has gained the professor's confidence. While they are doing that, I go out, get the car, pull up in front, and wait for them.

When we get back to the hotel, we discuss today's events. We decided to arrange to meet the professor again at the restaurant around 4:30 p.m. tomorrow instead of following him and running the risk of being seen.

The next day is a long day of waiting. We're anxious to get things started. My anxiety is caused by wishing I knew if he is making any progress on the Strontum-9 formula.

It's 4:30 p.m. now. The professor comes into the restaurant and joins Wong's table. They order from the menu. The waiter pours everyone a cup of tea. A few minutes later, he reaches for his briefcase, which is just enough time for Jess to administer the second vial. He takes out some photos and shows them around the table.

"Dr. Wong, is your family here with you?" Jess asks.

"No, I did not want to take my son out of school." He finishes his tea.

Dinner arrives, and everything is in place. Two hours later, dinner is over. I leave to get the car, and I wait in front.

The next morning, we follow the professor to work, park nearby, and just mill around like tourists. It isn't long before he comes back out with a colleague. They talk for a few minutes until his driver shows up. He gets in and drives off. We follow him from a safe distance, and sure enough, he goes home.

Now, the driver has to help him out of the car. We pull up, and Wong offers to help. Since they are both Chinese, the driver suspects nothing. Wong assures the driver that the professor is just exhausted and tell him to put him on the bed. He walks the driver to the door, tells him to be sure to pick him up tomorrow. When the driver leaves, Jess and I go inside to help Wong with the professor. On the way out, I take his briefcase. We do a slow, easy ride to the airport so that we don't arouse any suspicion.

When we arrive, I tell Jess to start the engines while Wong and I get the professor. While Wong is strapping him in, I go out, move the limo, and race back to the plane. Back inside and belted in, I call the tower for a clearance to Moscow, flight level 180. We get the clearance while Jess is taxiing into takeoff position.

We take off and climb to fl180.

"Okay, Jess, request a clearance to fl430. Once you get it, start climbing. Okay, now squawk 7600 and identify, but don't answer any more radio calls."

A few minutes later, we're leveling off at fl430.

"Shut off the transponder now. Now, turn right, heading 100 degrees; we're going to travel over Afghanistan, and some military planes just may come up and take a look at us. Keep an eye out, Jess. We should be intercepting an Austrian Global airliner any minute now."

"Okay, there it is, up ahead. I want you to descend to within 100 or 200 feet of it and to the right."

"Delaplane, who do you think I am? I can't do it; I'm not as good a pilot as you or Wong. Have Wong come up and take over."

She's never called me Delaplane before. She's scared.

"Inspector Stone, look at me, Wong is busy with the professor. If he gets out of those straps and opens the exit door, all of us are done for. Okay, I'll take the controls. I want you to keep a visual on that plane at all times."

She pauses, takes a deep breath.

"I have it, Jack, I'm sorry I lost my cool. I'm just scared."

She has calmed down now, so I let her take back the controls.

"So am I, if it makes you feel any better," I say. "But the scariest part is behind us now."

"I know you have your hands full, Jack, and thanks for restoring my confidence."

"We'll get through this. If anyone has sent any planes up to look around, they'll be looking up north, in Russia. Now, match that 747's cruise speed and set the auto pilot. That jet's going to Shanghai, and we're going to stay close all the way till we land. When you see its nose dip, it means he is leaving altitude, and we will do the same."

"When he crosses the outer marker, I'll take over, Jess. Everything will happen so fast then that I won't be able to talk you through it."

Jess has done a great job to get us down to the outer marker. I have to match her approach speed and gradually descend.

The 747 touches down. Now I have to touch down a short distance in front of where he touched down. About halfway up the runway, I turn off and head for the ramp to park. I set the parking brake to erase the flight data recorder and go to help Wong with the professor. We exit the plane, get into Wong's car, and head to the Shanghai hospital.

Once the high-level Chinese brass see him, they won't be sending anyone else there to help the Iranian government.

Jess says, "Let's go have a stiff drink some place. After that flight, I need one."

And Wong says, "Delaplane, I want you to give the professor's briefcase to Layne Industries. It may or may not contain anything, but my government needs to give this up."

"Thanks, my friend. I agree with you."

The next morning, Jess and I catch a flight back to Dulles to the U.S. When we arrive, I ask her to drop me off at Layne Industries. I take the familiar elevator up to Layne's office. Things have changed; there is a new secretary. She escorts me to his office.

"Jack Delaplane, come in. Let me introduce you to the new President of Layne Industries, my daughter, Nazanin."

"It's nice to meet you, Mr. Delaplane. Whatever working agreements you had with my dad will stay in place with me."

"The Trimeserall worked just like you said it would, and here is the Chinese professor's briefcase which Inspector Wong wanted you to have. I hope the Strontum-9 Affair is over."

I go back downstairs and hail a taxi to the No-name Bar. When I walk in, Xio Chen shouts, "John!"

I am glad to see her, too. I told her the Strontum-9 scare is finally over, but I couldn't say for how long.

She tells me the bar finally has its new name and directs my attention to the top-shelf drink area and a placard. It is: The Jade Dragon.

The Paraffin Caper

Anastasia Grant was finally seated for lunch in her favorite restaurant when a tall, young Chinese lady approached her table and said, "Hi, my name is Lin Cho; my employer would like a word with you."

Before Anastasia could answer her, a middle-aged Chinese man walked over and introduced himself. "My name is Leefong Yoon, and I must talk to you about a very urgent matter."

"Excuse me, but how do you know me?"

"I know that you work at the Bayou Agriculture Industry and that your company is working on a bacterium project that changes petroleum fuel to paraffin."

"And…?"

"Back in my country, our neighbor to the north is looking to start a lot of trouble. We are willing to pay a large fee for your help."

"How do I know this is not a setup?"

"Nothing will get traced back to you. Once you obtain and give us the bacterium, we will pay you cash, and you will never see us again. Here is a name and number for the Ottawa Mercantile Bank in Canada. Over the years, we have made lots of transactions through this bank. Again, I can assure you, this is not a setup."

Anastasia thought for a moment about the strangers' proposal and then reached into her purse, took out her cell phone, and dialed the number.

"Ottawa Mercantile Bank. This is Anita Douglas. How can I help you?" "This is Anastasia Grant, and I'm calling from New Orleans."

"I take it you have met with Mr. Yoon?"

As she ends the call, Mr. Yoon says, "Should you accept my offer, Ms. Grant, we will give you $2,000,000 for a demonstration."

"Okay, I'll accept your offer, but the demonstration can't be here. I'll do it in Boston. I'll give the address in Boston to Anita, and she will call you."

"Thank you very much; this will be a great help to my country." Yoon and the young lady quickly exited the restaurant.

Anastasia hurried back to her office and started making phone calls to arrange for pickup and delivery of the bacterium. The afternoon passed quickly, and all was arranged.

It was late Friday afternoon, and rush hour traffic was starting to build. Office buildings downtown had closed for the day, and the usual tourist groups had begun to descend on Bourbon Street. It was fairly quiet in the Cajun City of New Orleans. At peace? No.

A phone number was dialed hurriedly. "Hello?"

"Hi, I hope I'm not calling you too late." "No. You're not."

"Good, we're holding an auction in Boston tomorrow to raise funds, $2,000,000 to be exact. Can you meet me at the Hilton about 11:30 a.m. for a late breakfast?"

"Yes, sure."

"Thanks. Bye."

She made another call. "Are you on the road?"

"Yes, we will be at the gas station at 1:00 p.m."

With that done, she started packing a light overnight bag.

For me, it's rather quiet now; I was just heading home from dinner with my daughter, Jackie, at Mom's house. I usually spend Fridays finishing up my reports; this way, I don't have to play catch-up the following week. My daughter Jackie will be working with me starting Monday morning—as my partner. Now, I will have to be more careful with my cases and decisions; after all, she did learn to crawl before learning to walk. I don't want to put her in harm's way.

Since it was Friday night and still early, I stopped at the friendliest bar in town, the Woodbridge American Legion bar. As usual, the guys were still there.

"Hey, Delaplane, you haven't been in here since you got shot working that Strontum case. Have a beer on me. How've you been?"

"I came pretty close to having my ticket punched over there, but I still enjoy the work."

"You've been telling us for the past six years, 'One more year, then I'll retire.'"

"I still can't retire; I'm not rich like you guys."

I stayed for almost an hour, then went home to get some much-needed rest. Saturday, 9:05 a.m., and I was wide awake. Not that I wanted to be, but my phone was ringing.

"Hello."

"Good morning, Mr. Delaplane. My name is Phil Sunday. I work for Freedom Insurance, and I need your help on a very large insurance case. Can you come to my office this morning? We can discuss it in detail."

"Yes, sir, I should be there around 10:30 a.m."

I wrote down his address, and then I called Jackie. This could be a good first assignment for her. She picked me up at 10:00 a.m., and we drove to the Freedom Insurance Company offices. Because of all the Saturday morning shoppers, the traffic was heavy, and we got there a little late.

"Good morning Mr. Delaplane. I'm glad you could come on such short notice."

"This is my daughter, Jackie. She will be the main person handling this case," I said, "but I will be working with her."

"Here is a picture of Mr. Harry Saunders. He was delivering some packages to Layne Industry and claims that he slipped and fell in the lobby on a wet floor. Ruptured a few disks in his back, can't walk without a walker. He bought this policy with us five weeks ago."

Jackie spoke up before I could say anything.

"Mr. Sunday, cases like this could take some time. We will be glad to take your case, and I hope that early on we can find something to help close it. Most of the time, though, when people pull a scam like this, they go into hiding for several months."

"I know, but a $3,000,000 payout is not something that we get a thrill out of."

"Okay, we are not currently working on anything, so we will start now, and I'll keep you informed every chance I get."

"I took the liberty of making a folder of him for you which you can take with you. Here is a check for $300,000." Sunday handed Jackie a check.

Jackie took it, shook his hand, and requested a phone number, FAX number, and an e-mail for downloading information after hours.

Back in the car she said, "I hope you don't have plans for today. Let's go to Layne Industry; I want to talk with them."

"You're doing well," I told her. "I would do the same."

We took the elevator to the sixth floor where the receptionist escorted us into Layne's office.

"Mr. Delaplane, my name is Nazy Layne. We've met before."

"My name is Jackie Delaplane, and I will be working on cases with my Dad."

Nazy said, "Interesting, come in and sit down. I was just getting ready to call you about a delivery driver that slipped and fell in the lobby a few days ago. We just found out that he is suing us for $3,000,000 because of that fall. Our surveillance cameras show that he was here and down on the floor, but his claim doesn't match up with our cleaning times. I have the roll of film for that day's activities right here. My cleaning crew policy is to finish by 6:00 a.m."

"We would like to view that film; can we take it with us?" Jackie asked. She gave us the film and escorted us back to the receptionist, who in turn showed us to the elevator.

Back outside, Jackie said, "Let's see where Mr. Saunders lives. He may be living above his means and came up with this plan to get on easy street."

On the way, she deposited her first paycheck, and we continued on to check out the suspect's house.

It was a short 40-minute drive in spite of the Saturday traffic. Right away, she pointed out the steps up to the doorway. She drove around the block to view the back of the house; again, there were lots of stairs leading to the deck.

"On both sides of the house, there are too many steps for a person who can't walk to negotiate."

"You're reading my mind and you're thinking like a pro," I told her.

She said, "Let's go and analyze the film on my VCR." On the way, we went over together everything that we'd seen and heard.

In Boston, two ladies had finished their breakfast and were walking across the street to a gas station where a tanker truck was hooked up and ready to unload some fuel. The driver was inside talking to the manager and some customers.

Another driver emerged from a white van with a five-gallon gas can, climbed on top of the tanker, emptied his container of bacterium into the tanker, climbed back down, and retreated into the van.

About 15 minutes later, the driver came out of the station to unload some fuel.

•••

Driving home, Jackie asked, "What do you think, Dad? From the looks of his folder, he has family in Boston and Colorado."

"We just may have to split up—one of us takes Boston and the other, Colorado. But that could pose a problem; you're too new to take on a case alone."

"Okay, we don't split up; I can do this!"

"So you think he may go to one of those places to hide out until this is over?"

"That's a possibility, but he would have to get some hideous tattoo, or grow some weird hairstyle, so that when people do see him, they will only see the hair style and tattoo and not his true features."

"If he really is injured, then we lose."

She pulled into the driveway and we went inside.

"Hi Mom," I said, hugging my mother. "So far, she's doing great."

"Hi Grandma, we're going to look over some film; do you want to join us?"

"I'm in the middle of cooking dinner; maybe, if I get a break."

The first six viewings of the film didn't reveal anything to me. But Jackie seemed very intent and yelled, "Stop the tape! Back it up five seconds, back four more frames. Okay, play it in slow motion. Stop. Look at his right hand, there's something silver coming out of his hand."

"You're right."

Jackie said, "Keep going." It drops to the floor, bounces and rolls in front of him. "Stop, he's getting ready to step on it. Keep going, now he falls. Dad, he staged this whole thing."

"You're right. Look at the time on this film: three hours after the cleaning crew had finished their work. The floor is dry."

Back in Boston, the two ladies walked slowly towards the public phone that was nearest to the tanker truck. They could hear the driver yelling that the pumps weren't working. They watched him climb to the top of the tanker and shine his flashlight inside.

The driver began cursing and yelling that his tanker was filled with wax. He showed it to the station manager to confirm that he hadn't lost his mind.

The two ladies acknowledged the success of the show and walked over to the white van.

"Meet us at the warehouse for your pay-off at 16th and Pine at 3:00 p.m."

The van drove off, and the ladies walked away as the manager and the tanker driver were inside, reporting their problem.

At 16th and Pine, there were quite a few buildings here that the store merchants used to store their products for sale. A lot of the buildings were in need of repair with for sale signs on them.

The van driver and his partner went inside one of them to meet the two ladies.

"That was close; can we get paid now so that we can get out of the state?"

"Calm down; you're in the clear." Anastasia reached into her purse, took out two envelopes and dropped them onto the table. Before they could scoop them up, she took out her pistol and shot them both through the heart. The woman turned to her partner and said coolly, "That's $50,000 we can keep." She picked up the envelopes, and they both left. Then, the two ladies drove away from Boston, crossing over the Boston Inner Harbor. She ditched her gun.

Back in Virginia:

"Let's take him, in Dad."

"Not so fast; we'll need something a little more solid. Let's do some more surveillance on him first thing in the morning. You'll need to keep a travel bag handy with three or four days of clothing in case you have to travel on the spur-of-the-moment. You've done enough driving for today. I'll take a cab home."

"Okay, Dad, I'll pick you up in the morning."

After I got home, I packed three days' change of clothing, several cameras, and lots of film.

The next morning, Jackie called to tell me that she'd been watching the house since 7:00 a.m., and now, someone is coming out with luggage.

I said, "Follow them, no matter where they go. I'm on my way to watch the house." This is turning into a seven-day work week, and I do not like it. At 10:00 a.m., she called again to say she was on her way to Boston, and the lady she's following is now a man.

"Okay," I said. "Call me back when you get an address where he's staying." Just yesterday, I was thinking that she was too new at this. Her enthusiasm has just put egg on my face.

"Hello, Jung Lee, this is Delaplane. I need you to do me a favor." "Sure, what can I do?"

"I need you to file a flight plan to Boston for an 11:30 a.m. departure for me. Also, can you put my plane on the ramp? I'll be there in 45 minutes."

When I got to the Manassas, Virginia airport, Jung Lee was looking at me very hard, as if she wanted to ask me a question. She is such a beautiful lady.

Jackie called. "It's him, and he's staying with relatives here."

"You're doing an excellent job on this first case; you could handle it by yourself. Meet me at the Logan Airport in 55 minutes. I'm taking the Lear Jet."

"Okay, I've taken a lot of pictures already."

When I got there, she briefed me on everything that she'd done for the day.

"Come on, let's check in at the Hilton and eat lunch. Then we'll download your film on the computer and see what you have."

We walked into the restaurant, and my knees went weak. It was as if I had seen a ghost. From the back, Anita said, "Look what just came in, tall, dark and handsome."

Anastasia said, "Pretend that you don't know him. Let me do the talking."

I continued walking towards their table and said, "Lynette."

She said, "Excuse me, but I think you're confusing me with someone else. My name is Anastasia."

I began feeling awkward; I apologized and walk back to the front to be seated.

Anita asked, "Do you know him?"

"Yes, that's Jack Delaplane, a private detective. He killed my uncle, and I want him dead. The young lady he's with is his daughter. They must be working a case together."

Anita was silent and didn't ask any more questions. To me, the whole room went silent. Because of my embarrassment, we quickly finished our lunch and went upstairs to view the films. She still didn't have enough evidence for an unshakeable case yet.

I said, "We have to hit the streets again, and we'll stay on him until we get it."

Back in the restaurant, Anita had just gotten the confirmation that the $2,000,000 would be in the bank on Monday. They clicked their wine glasses to toast the good news.

Anastasia said, "With Delaplane already in Boston, he will hear the news and will want to poke his nose in it. Then I'll have him just where I want him."

I said goodnight to Jackie and adjourned to my room. My mind was in a fog because I kept thinking about Anastasia, the lady in the restaurant. She looked so much like Lynette. I poured myself a glass of cognac, took my shoes and shirt off, and lay down on the bed. My first thought was that hotel beds are not as comfortable as one's bed at home. An odd news flash came on the TV about how a tanker truck delivering fuel to a gas station was mysteriously filled with wax.

This got my attention but only for a short while because I laughed it off as a prank.

The next morning, I got up shortly after 7:00 a.m. and phoned Jackie to meet me in the restaurant for breakfast in 45 minutes. She got there shortly after I was seated.

"Good morning, Dad." "Morning. Did you sleep well?"

"Yes, and I have a plan on how to handle this. We will use two cars for our surveillance so that he can't tell he's being watched."

"That's a good plan, and I'm all for it."

She said, "I'll take the first watch, and you can stay here. I'll call you if I need you." We finished our breakfast, and she dropped me off at the car rental office.

I just knew she wanted to take the lead on this case and handle it herself. My mind kept wondering about this fuel tanker filled with wax, so I drove to the gas station to see it for myself. It was still there all right and with an inspection team also trying to figure out what happened.

After listening and watching for nearly an hour, I introduced myself. "Good morning gentleman, my name's Jack Delaplane, and I'm a private investigator. I have some friends back in Virginia who would be very much interested in analyzing that for you."

"Why not? We have a whole truck full of it. Cut him out a chunk of it, Fred, and tie it in this plastic bag." To me, this didn't seem like someone who went through the trouble of melting a lot of candles to achieve this. It was beginning to look sinister. I drove back to the hotel to wait for Jackie to call me to give her a break on the insurance case. She didn't call, so I went into the bar to take my own break. I knew what I was looking for, but as luck would have it, she was not here. It's late Sunday evening now, and Jackie didn't come up with anything new, so I called it a night.

The next morning, I got up and made a few phone calls before breakfast.

"Hello, this is Delaplane, and I would like to speak to Nazy Layne, please." I was put on hold while the receptionist made the connection.

"Good morning Mr. Delaplane. What can I do for you?"

"I'm not sure, but I'll try to explain it to you. Has there been anything on the news in Virginia about a fuel tanker truck in Boston being sabotaged?"

"Yes, I briefly listened to it while driving in to work."

"Is your Dad in today?"

"Yes, I'll transfer you."

"Good morning Jack, this is Allan. That fuel truck in Boston got my attention, too. We had a military contract to develop bacteria to convert fuel oil to wax some time ago. The bacteria strain that we created was not the fast-acting type they wanted. We ended up sub-contracting that task to a company in the southwest. I think it's located in New Orleans."

"If I brought you a sample of that wax, could you analyze it?"

"I sure can. Are you involved in that tanker issue in Boston the news media is buzzing about?"

"No, I'm not. Something just doesn't look right to me. It's mid-morning now, so I'll meet with you at 1:00 pm."

After we hung up, I called Jackie to tell her that I was flying back to Manassas for a meeting. I will contact her later.

In New Orleans, a number is hastily dialed.

"Hello, Ottawa Mercantile Bank, this is Anita Douglas."

"Hi Anita, this is Anastasia Grant, do you have a name and number for me?"

"Yes, but they want a sample of the formula."

"No, that is not the deal! The plan is $80,000,000 in exchange for the formula. We can't possibly do another large-scale demo. You saw how the media got on the last one in Boston."

"Okay, when you set up the meeting, I want to be there with you." "Okay, bye."

I quickly packed my overnight bag, checked out of the hotel and rushed to Logan Airport. I returned the rental car and ran to my plane to file my flight plan.

"Logan Tower, this is N1976NL, and I would like to file a flight plan to Manassas Regional Airport. Cruising altitude Fl380, airspeed 480, and I'm requesting immediate departure."

"N1976NL, this is Logan Tower taxi to Runway 18 and hold."

Before I got to the runway, I had my departure clearance. Halfway down the runway, I lifted off and gave it a steep climb.

A short while later, I parked my plane at the Manassas Airport. I went inside the terminal. "Hi Jung Lee, can you get someone to top off the main for me and put it on my bill?"

"Yes, sir, I'll take care of it for you."

"I don't know what I'd do without you, lady."

I got into my car and drove to 1608 Greenwich Way in Manassas. During the trip, I'm trying to piece together possible reasons why the military wanted Layne Industry to develop a bacteria that changes fuel oil to paraffin.

It's just not coming to me.

When I get there, I go up to Suite 608, and the secretary escorts me into Layne's office.

"Delaplane, come in. We were just talking about this incident in Boston that seems to have captured your interest."

"That's good because I can't figure out why the military wanted such a bacteria."

"That's any easy question; they wanted to contaminate the enemy's fuel supply. Tanks can't move, planes can't fly, and their ships can't sail. The country is helpless."

"Mr. Layne, this country has a major problem on its hands. Some person or persons just put on a demonstration in Boston to show what they are capable of."

I handed him the plastic bag and said, "This is what they gave me out of that tanker truck. Can you analyze it and determine where the bacterium was produced?"

"This looks like a bacterium that was used to digest the hydrocarbons in the fuel. This is very similar to our undertaking when we contracted that job out to The Bayou Agriculture Industry in New Orleans. The weather is perfect there for year-round growth. I'll give it to our lab, and let them break it down. Hopefully, I can give you an answer in 48 hours."

I turned to Nazy and said, "Jackie is handling your case on Mr. Saunders. He's left town and is staying in Boston. She will continue her surveillance of him until she gets some solid proof."

"Okay, that's good, but you're working with her and that's what took you to Boston?"

"Yes, I am, and what I've stumbled upon now could be disastrous for this country."

Mr. Layne said, "Why would you think that? They could have been just testing it."

"If they were just testing it, they would have used a smaller container and not a full truck. We have to find that formula, and fast. If it ends up in some rogue country's hands and they decide to use it on our fuel supplies, this country is shut down. In the meantime, I'll assemble a team to help me find this formula. Call me when you have something for me."

I said my goodbyes to them and quickly exited the room.

In New Orleans, Anastasia made another phone call, very brief. "We're ready."

Before I get to my car, my phone rang. "Hi, Dad, where are you?"

"I had to come back to Manassas for something very important. How are you doing on the Saunders case?"

"I shot a lot of film today of him before he went to the tattoo parlor and afterwards. He's even changed his hair color."

"You did great. Why don't you pack up and come back, and I'll meet your plane at Dulles."

Jackie arrived at Dulles late that afternoon, and I briefed her on where we stood with the paraffin case on the drive home. Over the next few hours, she finished her report on Mr. Saunders and then Xeroxed copies for Mr. Sunday and Layne Industry.

"You got lucky on this case," I said. This was a young kid, new in the business of trying to run a scam like this and who didn't have the patience to wait it out. Sometimes, it takes weeks, or months, before you would get something substantial to go on."

In the meantime, I placed a call to an old friend. "Hello, this is Sam Delaware."

"Hi, Sam, this is Delaplane. How are you? I'm calling to find out if you can help me out on a case."

"Sure. I'll be glad to work a job with you. I'll give you a call when I arrive in Virginia tomorrow morning."

After dinner, I said goodnight to the family and headed over to the Jade Dragon to see how Xio Chen was doing with the expanded business. From the looks of the packed parking lot, business had almost doubled; she was right again. What a lady.

When I walked in, Ahn Lee and two other ladies were working the bar. Xio came out from the office to collect drop money for bookkeeping from the registers. On her way back, she brought me into the office.

She says, "We have a full staff, everyone is being taken care of, and I love it." She kissed me, very close. "I love you, John." I kissed her back, just as close; then I walked over to the file cabinet, reached for the bottom drawer. She stopped me. She walked over to the wall cabinet and opened the door to show me where my stash was kept.

With this "Paraffin Caper" weighing on my mind, I only stayed a short while; I said good night to Xio and headed home early.

The next morning, shortly after breakfast, my doorbell rang, and I answered it.

"Sam, come on in." Over coffee, I briefed him on what I knew about the paraffin case.

"You don't know their motive, do you, Jack?"

"No, I don't, but they want somebody to know they can make it and use it in a destructive manner."

My phone rings. "Hi, this is Delaplane."

"Mr. Delaplane, this is Nazy Layne. Can you come down to my office?

We may have something on the 'Paraffin Case' that you brought in."

"I'm on my way." On the way, Jackie called, and I told her to meet us at Layne's office.

It was nearly 11:00 a.m. when we arrived; we all took the elevator upstairs. Once in her office, Jackie spoke up first.

"Here is my report on Mr. Saunders, along with some photos. I've made duplicates for Freedom Insurance, also."

"Thank you so much for what you've done. That's one headache that I'm glad to be without."

"Now, here is the real headache. The paraffin bacteria that we've analyzed is a quality grade grown in the southwest. We are certain that it came from the Bayou Agriculture Industry. I don't know of any contacts there that may be of any help to you, but we at Layne Industry will pay you for your services."

"I have no idea what to look for, but whatever is going on, it must be stopped."

The three of us agreed to take on the paraffin case together as we left Nazys' office.

Jackie said, "Let's take the Lear Jet to New Orleans. I'll pilot."

Trying to devise a plan was out because we didn't know what we would be facing. I called our flight plan in, requesting a 1:00 p.m. departure. In the past, Sam and I had worked together on some spur-of-the-moment cases that had taken some patience to wait around and see what was going on. It also took some luck to capitalize on a break when we saw it.

It was a little after 4:00 p.m. when we arrived, picked up our rental car, and went off to find the Bayou Agriculture Industry. With all of the posted directions, it wasn't hard to find. A lot of employees were leaving, so we opted to snoop around the main Admin building. Before we reached the building, I stopped abruptly. I saw two ladies getting out of a car; I recognized them from my trip in Boston. Another car pulled in beside them, and two Asian men got out, carrying two large travel bags. They weren't dressed in business attire. I pointed out the two ladies to Jackie, and she recognized them, too. The two Asians with them piqued my curiosity.

Sam said, "This does not look like a business meeting or a date. Let's tag along—this could be a break for us."

The building they entered had no surveillance cameras outside, and all the employees were leaving, so we weren't sending up any red flags to arouse anyone's curiosity. We watched from a distance as they went in and proceeded to an office in the middle of the building as the lighting indicated.

After a short deliberation, we decided to go in. As we slowly made our way through the entrance, we heard loud talking, as if they were in disagreement, followed by what sounded like gun shots. I grabbed Bedilia out from under my arm and headed for the office where the shots came from.

I yelled, "Jackie, don't go inside."

In a flash, Sam rushed past me and kicked the door open, instantly drawing fire. As I rushed in behind him, I saw one of the two ladies on the floor with a bullet wound to the heart. From across the room and slumped behind a desk, the other lady saw me and called out, "John."

I froze because I recognized her voice. She knew my name, but in Boston, I was a total stranger to her. One of the men was trying to work his way behind her, but I shot him before he could get there. The familiar sound of her voice left my head in a fog; I rushed to get to her. The other man, seeing this, poked his head up over the desk, and Sam quickly took him down.

I went over to her and said her name. "Lynette."

She managed a smile and said, "I have to tell you something. Lynette is my sister; her real name is Linda Grant. When she worked at Layne Industry, she couldn't use her real name for fear of kidnappings, extortion, and the like. After we found out that you killed our uncle, I wanted you killed. When you showed up in Boston a few days ago, I knew this would get your attention, and you would jump on this case. You were supposed to trail these two out of the country, get into a foreign shootout, and get killed."

"Professor Keatings was your uncle?"

"Yes, and Linda has a boutique in Manassas."

Sam said, "Delaplane, look at this. It's some kind of formula in a folder, and there are bags of money. What are we going to do with this?"

"We're working for Layne Industry, so we'll just take it back to Layne, and let him sort it all out."

Jackie came over and said, "An ambulance is on the way along with the police."

Before the woman died, she had told me her name was Anastasia Grant.

So, the purpose of the Paraffin Caper was to lure me into it, and being outnumbered, I would be killed. Also, they could make a ton of money.

I told Sam and Jackie to take the bags of money out to the car before the police arrived. I wanted to come up with an alibi for Anastasia so that she wouldn't be remembered as a traitor.

"Hi, I'm Lieutenant Wilson of the New Orleans Police Department." "My name is Jack Delaplane, and…"

"The world-famous Inspector Delaplane? I have read so much about you. It is an honor to meet you."

"This is Sam Delaware from…"

"Wow, two famous detectives. This is an honor."

"This is my daughter, Jackie, who's also working this case with us." "Lieutenant Wilson, we were hired by Layne Industry to investigate the possible theft of a U.S. Government formula."

"My guess is that these two ladies walked in by surprise on these two crooks searching for the formula."

"The lady over here has family in Virginia. Can you have the coroner ship the bodies back, and I'll take care of the bill. Here's my card."

"The rest of them aren't going to believe me when I tell them about you, so can you stop in at the precinct and say hi to the group?"

"Sure, we'll do that for you."

He believed my story. In fact, it was almost as if I was talking to Lieutenant Gallini.

It was almost 10:30 p.m. when we got back to Manassas. On the way home, we stopped at the Jade Dragon.

Jackie said, "I'll close the report for Layne Industry, so you can sleep in tomorrow."

"You've done a great job all week on these cases, and I'm proud of you."

Meanwhile, back in New Orleans, the doctors were frantically working to save the life of one of the surviving ladies who was shot.

Back in Manassas, as we were walking into the Jade Dragon, Jackie said, "I can handle a Beretta."

Once inside Xio Chen greeted us, and I introduced her to Sam.

"You have a nice lounge here, Delaplane. You should just manage it, and stop putting your life on the line stopping crooks."

"When I first started out in the business, I had a very small place, and it was always packed. Xio Chen stayed on me about expanding, so I just let her do her thing, and now it's still packed."

"I've thought about retiring many times, but I just can't seem to walk away from the excitement of it all."

"I know what you mean; all I know is the detective business, and I never made any investments to keep me occupied when I retire. I've managed to set some money aside, but it's the excitement that keeps me going."

Later, Jackie dropped Sam off at my place. She thanked him for his work on the case and said she would put a check in the mail for his efforts.

Sam got into his car and headed off to the airport. I went inside the house, poured a glass of cognac, and went out onto the deck.

It's May 25. It's been almost two months since we've finished the Paraffin Caper, and I haven't taken on any new cases, mainly because I've wanted to take a long vacation. I had purposely dragged the idea out so that I could be sure Jackie was comfortable in the business. She wanted to work a divorce case to know what it entailed. She even worked with my friend Lt. Vic Gallini on a couple of robberies. She concluded that Vic will always be the same; he just doesn't close out any cases.

•••

The Setup

For the past three weeks, I'd been trying to plant some grass on the sloping hill in my back yard. Last year, I tried it, and nothing grew. After this effort and nothing grows, I'll just let a lawn service take care of this yard work.

Early the next morning, a phone rings across town. "Hello?"

"Hi, I haven't been able to drop the folder. He may not go to the airport." "He will; he's been working with his daughter to be sure she can take over for him. I know you don't want to get involved, but I need your help.

"I'm still not healed up."

"Okay, I'll do it. I just want to hurry up and get it over with."

It was now 1:30p.m., and I'd made all the necessary arrangements for my trip to Switzerland for a month, two weeks in Hong Kong, two weeks in Australia, three weeks in Hawaii, and back home.

After completing my itinerary, I got into the car and headed over to the Friendliest Bar in Town to hang out with the gang. The drive was only 25 minutes, and I didn't pay any attention to the SUV that followed me all the way and parked about 40 yards from me.

Across town a phone ran. "Hello?"

"Hi. He's going into the Woodbridge American Legion." "Good, I'll handle it from here. Bye."

The phone rang in the bar. Big Al, the bartender, answered, "American Legion."

"Hi, my name is Barbara Story of the Washington Paper. Delaplane will be coming in shortly, and I can't be seen near him. Can you give me a call if he starts bashing my paper while he's there?"

"I sure will."

"Thank you so much, and here is my number."

"Look who just walked in, guys. Are you lost, Delaplane? You haven't been here in months."

"I know you all missed me, and I'm going to make you miss me even more. Starting Saturday, I'm taking three months off and travel the world." The bartender opened a beer and placed it in front of me. I gave him two dollars to pay for it.

"I've always wanted to spend a real vacation in Switzerland, so that will be my first stop, for a month. The only way to see a country is to live as the locals do."

After an hour of just small talk, the bartender went into the office and called Ms. Story.

"Hello, this is Barbara Story."

"Hi, you asked me to call you about Delaplane. He's just going on and on about his vacation starting this Saturday. Sorry I couldn't be of any help to you."

"Oh, but you have been. It's good to know that he's no longer bashing my paper. Thank you, and goodbye." She quickly called the SUV driver to tell her that Delaplane's travel date was set for Saturday and to leave before she was seen.

By nightfall, the plan for Saturday was in place, and the clock was ticking.

After my third beer, I left the bar and headed over to see my mom. We spent the evening making small talk over dinner and Jackie showing her enthusiasm over how much she likes her job and saying that she would be fine while I'm on vacation.

"I just thought of something. Jessie Stone is a very good backup for you if you need someone. She and I have worked a lot of cases together over the years."

"Okay, I'll remember that."

"She will be fine, Jack," said Mom. "I remember when you first started in the business and how excited you were. Hold on a minute here; you have something on your mind, don't you?"

"Yes, I think I've reached a point where I'm starting to care too much about my clients. When you start caring too much, this is not the business to be in."

"What are you going to do?"

"I don't know. At one point, I thought I was ready to settle down with Xio Chen. Then she called it off."

"Well, take this vacation time and rest, then come back with a clear mind, and you'll be as good as new."

"Thanks, Mom. I'll stop by again before I leave. Goodnight." It was a short drive home.

I went inside and poured a glass of cognac.

•••

"Grandma, ever since we finished that job in New Orleans, he's been very moody. It's as if he has seen a ghost."

"That would be my guess also, but he has to find out on his own."

"Two years ago, he was seeing Lynette, and for some, reason she disappears."

"Now Xio Chen changes her mind and doesn't want to get married."

"That's it. They both feel that Dad's work is too dangerous, and don't want to end up widows; also, they don't want to come between Dad and his work. Grandma, I think you and I would be great working on a case together."

It was almost midnight when I decided to lie down.

The next two days were uneventful; time passed quickly. It was now Saturday morning, and I took a cab to the airport. After the slow process through the ticket line and the security checkpoint line, I proceeded to the lounge area and awaited my flight.

Downstairs, a lady called out to one of the baggage handlers, "Are you Mr. Davis? I was told to come here and speak only to you."

"Yes, I am. What can I do for you?"

"My boss forgot his construction plans, and it would be a wasted trip for him without them. His name is John Delaplane."

"There's his luggage, over there. Come into my office while we open it." She stuffed the folder into the luggage, handed the baggage handler a $100 bill, and quickly exited the terminal.

The process of going through the security check line was slow, but it had to be done. I boarded the plane, found my seat in first-class, and put away my carry-on bag. After fastening my seat belt, I thought about how odd I felt traveling without Bedilia under my arm. The thought was short-lived, though; I'm now on a much-needed vacation.

I felt the plane in motion now, moving away from the terminal to the hold area to await our departure time. It seemed like forever—I was anxious to get away.

We were finally airborne. The captain had turned off the "fasten seatbelt" sign. The stewardess came over, and I asked her for a glass of cognac. I savored the first sip and commenced to read the newspaper. It was now 11:30 a.m.; the flight stewards were starting to serve lunch. After they served the first-class passengers, they took the flight crew their meals. After 45 minutes, they returned to the cockpit to retrieve the flight crew's dishes. Within seconds, a stewardess returned to the cabin, a panicked look on her face. I rushed to her and asked, "What's wrong?"

"The flight crew is unconscious!"

I looked at her name tag and said, "Veronica, we don't want a panic on our hands, now; calm down. I am a pilot, come back into the cockpit with me. Let's see what's going on. We are on autopilot, so there's no need to panic. Go back into first class and move the first four rows of people back a little farther; then come back up here, and help me."

The passengers in the first-class section were starting to panic after seeing what was going on; she was able to calm them a little.

After a few minutes, she returned to the cockpit.

"Now, help me move the flight crew into those vacated rows. Now, Veronica, I want you to check the passenger manifest to see if there is a pilot on board. It should be noted as Pass Rider. If you find one, bring him up here. Now, go."

While she was checking the manifest, I sat down in the left seat to familiarize myself with this make and model.

Veronica walked over to Row 26 and addressed the gentlemen in the aisle seat. "Excuse me, sir, and are you a pilot?"

"Yes, a retired pilot."

"Good. Sir, will you follow me to the cockpit?"

She opened the door, and they walked in. I introduced myself to him, "Hi, my name is Jack Delaplane, and I'm a Lear 86 pilot."

"My name is John Sheehy, and I'm a retired Eastern pilot; I can fly the A330."

"That is great news."

"Okay, Delaplane. You sit in the right seat, and I'll sit in the left. We will get through this."

Captain Sheehy quickly glanced over: the glare shield; center instrument panel; flight control unit; and the six cathode ray tubes that provide guidance for control and monitoring of the aircraft all appeared to be functioning normally. Also, the auto pilot was engaged in navigation mode, tracking the pre-takeoff flight plan. He asked the flight steward to see if there was a doctor on board, engaging the PA system.

"Ladies and Gentlemen, this is Captain Sheehy. The flight crew has been incapacitated, and I have taken command of the aircraft. We are not being hi-jacked, nor are we in any danger, so please remain in your seats. Thank you."

Veronica returned to tell us that there are neither doctors nor other pilots on board. She reached to take away the flight crew's dishes, but I prevented her from doing so.

"Captain Sheehy, I could smell a light odor of Valerian when I first entered the cockpit. The dishes can be checked later for evidence. We must get back to Dulles. For now, just between you and me, whoever did this works in the in-flight kitchen, and they may be planning to drug more flights."

Realizing the importance of returning to Dulles, he tuned the number one Radio Management Panel to VHF frequency 121.5. He selected the VHF 1 and started transmitting a distress call.

"Pan, Pam, Pan this is First Air Flight 867 requesting message relay to New York Oceanic."

"This is US Air Flight 881; go ahead with your message." Right away, I picked up the Sat Phone and called Jessie Stone. "Hello, Jess, this is Delaplane, I need your help."

"Okay, you got it."

I explained the situation to her and the importance of avoiding the news media. I also told her that she must convince the bosses at Langley and the FBI that I and Captain Sheehy, a retired pilot, are in the cockpit and that the plane was not being hi-jacked. I also told her to bring Vic in on it.

In about 45 minutes, we got the clearance to return to Dulles with two escort jets. We were scrutinized by Homeland Security all the way back to verify that we were not terrorists. Four hours later, we were on the ground, and Captain Sheehy was told to leave the plane on the runway.

The medical team hurried onboard with some FBI agents. Veronica, the flight steward, escorted them to the front of first class. Sheehy and I exited the cockpit and greeted them. One look from the FBI agent, and he said, "Delaplane, at first I didn't believe them."

I said, "Let's back them on who they say they are and bring them back to Dulles."

While the medical team was tending to the flight crew, I took the agents into the cockpit and showed them the food containers of the flight crew. I bent down and sniffed them. While they were putting on latex gloves, I said, "Agent Johnson, I don't know how accurate your nose, is but I can still smell Valerian in these dishes."

"I can't tell, but I'll have the lab check it out."

"Okay, if my suspicions are confirmed, then you better investigate the in- flight cooks because they may be planning more of this."

The medical team evacuated the flight crew. The plane is then towed to the terminal, and everyone is allowed to deplane.

I was met inside by Jess and Vic, and we head to the baggage terminal as I'm briefing them on what happened.

"Vic, when I asked that you be here, I wanted you to take over the investigation of the in-flight cooks. It would have been a big feather in your cap and quite possibly you could have made Captain. Maybe, on one of my upcoming cases, I'll help you reach that goal."

As I reached to get my baggage, two customs agents stopped me. "Are you John Delaplane?"

"Yes, I am, why?"

They took my bags and escorted us into their office. There they opened my luggage and find a folder stamped "Property of Layne Industry."

"Mr. Delaplane, you are under arrest for possession and attempted sale of government documents." At that time, Mr. Layne was escorted in to verify the documents were his. All four of us are dumb-founded by the allegations. Layne examined at the folder with a questioning look on his face. It's the Strontum-9 folder. I'm turned over to Lt. Gallini to be escorted to the Manassas jail. I turned to Jess and said, "Call my lawyer, Dawn Starke. Tell her to meet me there, but I don't want bail posted yet." I leaned over and whispered to Jess to look at the folder. They handed Vic the folder to hold as evidence.

Layne said, "Vic, this is a top secret file. I have to take it back to for safe keeping. If you need it to check for prints, you will have to go through our corporation, and we'll bring it down to you." Vic slid the folder into his briefcase; he closed it and left the airport.

It was a quiet ride back to Manassas with Vic. He knew I wasn't going to talk about what just went down. However, we did manage some small talk. I guess, in their own minds, Vic and Layne knew I didn't do this, but we had to go through the formalities. Jess and Starke met me there and waited while Vic did the paperwork on me. Afterwards, he escorted us into an interview room where we could talk in private. I told them that I wanted to spend the weekend in jail so that it would make the nightly news and that whoever did this could relax and feel that they had nailed me. I told them to post my bail on Tuesday and that I wanted a brief meeting with Layne in his office that afternoon.

"Okay, when you want out, just say the word, and you're free to go," said Vic.

"Thanks, Dawn, for coming here. I'll stay in touch. I'll see you on Tuesday, Jess."

That night, one of the guards came by to tell me that I made the nightly news and that it was "on all the channels." Across town, however, there was one happy face that seemed to be ecstatic after hearing the news.

"I got you, now, Delaplane. You will pay for what you did to me—for a long time!"

The weekend passed rather slowly; I was able to formulate my ideas as to what I wanted to do. When you know you're in here for the weekend, it's easier to take. When you're here for years, it's got to be hell.

Tuesday morning came. Jess was there to pick me up.

"I want to stop by and say hi to Mom and Jackie before we get started."

"Okay, I've already set up the appointment at Layne Industry for 1:00 p.m."

Shortly after noon, we headed downtown for the meeting. "Jack, come in. I'm glad to see you. Have a seat."

"Thanks for giving me the time. As you know, I can't talk about what happened over the weekend. The reason I'm here is to ask if I can take that folder home with me to run some tests on it for prints."

He didn't balk at bringing me the folder because I was the one who went halfway around the world to bring it back to him.

"Mr. Layne, this is the Strontum-9 folder. You and I both know that it's useless.

"If I was going to steal a folder, it would have been the Strontum-7 folder. Now whoever took this and planted it in my luggage had no idea that Strontum-7 existed."

"If you feel that you can lift some prints off of it, by all means, take it. If anyone else comes around looking for it, I'll stall them. Vic has already looked it over yesterday morning, but he gave it back right away."

"Thanks, I'll get back to you as soon as I can."

I took the Strontum-9 folder home with me to better analyze for prints. Vic and his department had analyzed it, but I just didn't trust the quick work they would have done. I always believe in looking for the not-so-obvious. The next three days went by pretty slowly because I had to lift prints and file pages. It was a very slow, one-man process. I was finding prints that were large in diameter, which suggested to me they were from a man. There were also a lot of smudged prints. On Friday morning, I ate a light breakfast and started working again. It was late afternoon, and all I was coming up with were the same type of prints. I was starting to feel like I'd been roughed-up but not defeated. I stopped what I was doing and headed over to the Jade Dragon. I needed a change of pace.

When I walked in, Xio Chen greeted me with a hug and a kiss. We weren't romantically involved any longer, but I still cherished her friendship.

"John, you've lost some weight. This trouble spot that you're in now is getting the best of you."

"I've been under a lot of stress trying to clear my name and reputation. Some person or persons have managed to set me up, and I don't have much time to find them before the trial date."

She mixed a glass of cognac and ginger ale and placed it in front of me. All along, she listened intently as I told her where I stood on the investigation.

When I had finished, she said, "Someone must know they can't kill you, so now they are trying their next plan, to destroy you."

I took a slow sip of my drink. What she just said kept echoing in my head.

"Xio, you are beautiful and brilliant. Now, if someone came in here to rob you silently, who would it be?"

"It would be someone whom I trust and someone that I didn't have to watch."

"That's it! I've been so consumed with finding an obvious past enemy that I forgot to look for 'a friend with an axe to grind.' Thank you; you're such a gorgeous lady." I leaned forward, kissed her, and left.

I hurried home and ran the folder under my blue image resonator scan. At the lower right-hand corner of the first page, I found a print. It was smaller, thinner, and retrievable. In the same area on each page of the document I was able to lift a print. It was late when I completed the sweep for prints; I didn't know any contacts in Vic's office that I could trust. I was very tired when I went to bed.

The next morning, I headed for Manassas Airport. Just as I got there, Jung Lee was getting out of her car. She ran over and gave me a long kiss. "John, I was hearing so much about the trouble you were in, and I was so worried. Are you all right?"

"Yes, I'm fine. Thanks for asking."

"Are you going flying today? Take me with you. I can help with the flying there and back."

"I have to go to New Orleans to check up on an old case."

"I'm coming with you; they have plenty of help here for today. I can see that this job you're on now has really taken a toll on you."

"You're right; this one does have me in a tailspin. I'm just grasping at straws. Most of the thugs I've had to deal with are still locked up or they're pushing up daises. Some person or persons got into Layne Industry, took that folder out of his safe-keeping, and planted it in my luggage."

"It's okay now. You're in no shape to be flying alone, and I'm here to help you."

Four hours later, we landed in New Orleans. We took a cab to the hospital to see the coroner. It had been quite a while since the shooting here, and I didn't remember the exact date. The coroner looked back through his files, and sure enough, he found what I was looking for. From there, we went over to the Bayou Agriculture Industry for the rest of my questions. No such luck.

It was late in the afternoon, and Jung Lee wanted to play tourist since she'd never been to New Orleans. We went to Bourbon Street, shopped, ate, and toured some more. She called a hotel to make a reservation for us while I purchased several umbrellas to take back to Virginia. We were in walking distance of the hotel, so we walked back she was very close on my arm. We walked into the lounge, and I ordered cognac and ginger ale for us. She reached over and touched my hand, and said, "John, this is the best time I've had in a long time. I don't want it to end."

"Jung Lee, my job is not the safest job around. One day I could go to work, and they would bring me home in a pine box."

"That's okay. I'll take that chance, and whatever time is given me to be with you."

We took the elevator up to our room; I pulled her close and kissed her as we opened the door. Once inside, she hurriedly unbuttoned my shirt, raking my back with her nails in her excitement. Jung Lee was very beautiful, fit, and energetic. We shared a slow, deep kiss, "I love you, Jung Lee."

"John, I've waited years for you to tell me that. I love you, too," she responded.

Our love for each other played well into the wee morning hours. Then we both fell asleep. It was almost 9:00 a.m. when we awoke, but we stayed in bed until late in the morning. We showered and dressed, then went downstairs to check out and eat breakfast. We took a taxi to the airport, and Jung wanted the captain's seat so that she could do the flying. I'd known her a long time; she's flown my plane on numerous occasions, and I thought she could handle it as well as I. We shared a lot of talk flying back, and just like that, the three-and-a-half hour flight was over.

While walking towards our cars, I told Jung Lee that I wanted to close out this case against me by tomorrow and that I would see her afterwards. She kissed me and said okay, and we both left the airport.

On the way home, I stopped at The Friendliest Bar in Town. Big Al, the bartender, placed a beer in front of me and said, "Just before you went on your vacation, a lady called here and wanted to know what you were talking about in here. I told her that you were planning your vacation, and she was very happy about that."

"You know, Al," I said, "I think this lady is the one who set me up for all this grief that I'm having. Thanks for the information."

My next move would be a gamble, but most importantly, the timing had to be right. After I got home, I was too nervous to eat a big meal, so I went to the kitchen and fixed some soup and a sandwich. After I ate, there was nothing more I could do until I ran the prints through the police fingerprint file. I poured a glass of cognac and went out onto the deck. I thought about Jung Lee, and I called her. Over several calls, we talked until almost midnight and then I went to bed.

The next morning, I got up, ate breakfast, and arrived at Vic's office sharply at 9:00 a.m.

"Good morning, Dan. Is Vic in?"

"Yes, he is, but he's in with the Captain."

"Oh, can I run a couple of prints through your files so I can close out a case?"

"Sure, but don't let him catch you, he'll go nuts."

"Thanks, I'll be quick." I ran the prints through, and inside of 30 minutes, I got matches on them. As I was leaving I said to Dan, "Stop by the Jade Dragon sometime, and I'll buy you a drink."

"Ok, I sure will. See you, Delaplane."

It was mid-morning as I quickly drove to downtown Manassas to visit a ladies' boutique. As I walked in, there she was, rearranging a display. I walked over to her. She had a look of surprise, or rather, shock on her face; I couldn't tell which. In a way, I was glad to see her.

"Hi, it's been a long time." I said.

"Yes, it has been. This is the best place to disappear from a man and still be in plain sight."

I stopped her from turning away from me and looked into her eyes. "I'm sorry for what happened to your sister in New Orleans last year. I closed out that case with their police department to make it look as if she was a hero even though she was shot and killed by the thugs that broke into her office." I still haven't told her the full story, why I stopped in. She slowly backed away and started walking towards her office. I followed. She opened the door and told me to come in. When I entered her office, I was surprised but then again I wasn't because of the fingerprints I found that morning. "Hello, Anastasia, I thought you were dead."

"Well, I guess it's true, a cat does have nine lives."

"I'm glad to see that you're alive and here. I came here to have a discussion with Linda, but now I can share it with both of you."

"For the past two weeks, I've been trying to find the person who framed me with the Strontum-9 folder from Layne Industry. I went over every inch of those papers, day and night. Just this morning, I found both your prints on them. A stranger could not have gotten into Layne Industry without being questioned. Since Linda worked there, it was easy for her to mill around until she found what she was looking for. She didn't want to do this, but you talked her into it. She didn't know that the Strontum-9 folder was useless, and neither did you."

Linda nervously sat down in the chair behind her desk and started to cry. Anastasia quickly walked over to her to comfort her and started to cry. I waited until they both composed themselves.

"Wait, ladies, hear me out, and don't say anything yet, please. For what I'm about to say I will be wrestling with my conscience for a long time. Neither one of you will survive in a jail for any length of time. I spent four days in there, and I know firsthand what it's like. First of all, I am not the heartless person that you think I am. I will give you two options: we can continue this and proceed to trial, and 10 times out 10, you will be found guilty and my reputation is cleared."

"I've also found some smudged prints and others that matched Lt. Gallini. After I show him these, he will be more than glad to close this case as insufficient evidence and Layne Industry will also go along with it."

I called Layne's office and told him that I wanted an urgent meeting with him. Then I called Vic and told him to meet us at Layne Industry. Both of the ladies faces showed signs of relief, and they both thanked me for my generosity. As I was walking towards the door, Anastasia followed me.

"John, I would like very much to be your friend." She extended a hand to me. I accepted her handshake and said, "I would like that very much."

From there, I went immediately to 1608 Greenwich Way and met with Layne and Vic. I laid the folder and prints on the table in front of Vic.

"You ran this folder through your print file, Vic, and you didn't find any of my prints on it. What you did find was your own." I looked up at Layne; he wasn't surprised. He knew where I was going with this meeting, and he knew I wouldn't throw my friend, Vic under a bus.

It was a short one-hour meeting. I hated to put my friend, Vic, on the spot like that, and I had already promised Anastasia and Linda that they wouldn't do any time. It was up to Vic now not to call my bluff. He quickly called the Justice Office to say that the case against me was dropped, and Mr. Layne concurred.

"Gentlemen, before I came over here, I had wiped this folder clean because I couldn't believe you would have done this to me, Vic."

"Thanks, Delaplane, I have no idea how my prints got on that folder."

"You need to start watching your back, Vic; someone may be trying to keep you from making captain."

"I'm sorry I took up so much of your time, Mr. Layne."

"That's quite all right, I'm glad this is cleared up because all three of us have been friends for a long time."

Vic and I went over to the Jade Dragon and had a beer to show that our friendship was still in place, and he said that he personally would write up the report to close it out. Somehow, I believed him. After we left, I made another call.

"Hello, Jung Lee, how are you?"

"John, I'm doing great for having a so-so kind of day."

"How would you like to have dinner tonight? What time can you get off?"

"I would love to have dinner tonight. I'm leaving right now to get ready."

"I will pick you up at 5:00 p.m., then. Bye."

I went home and poured a glass of cognac, checked my mail and my e- mail, and went out onto the deck. I didn't tell her that we were having dinner at my mom's because I knew Mom would call me and tell me to come over anyway. I went back inside and, sure enough, the phone rang; it was Mom. I showered, got dressed, and went over to pick up Jung Lee. She greeted me at the door with a hug and a kiss.

"I'm so excited; I haven't seen you in a few days, and I knew you were busy closing this case out."

"You look so gorgeous!"

We got in the car and off we went. Not once did she ask where we were going. Twenty minutes later, we pulled into Mom's driveway.

"Wow, John, this is such a big house. Why didn't you tell me that we are house guests?"

"I wanted to surprise you. We're having dinner with my Mom and my daughter." She was all smiles. She walked over to my mom, extended her hand and said, "Hello, Mrs. Delaplane, I'm so glad to finally meet you."

"Well, Jung Lee, I am very glad that I've finally met you also." She gave her a big hug. "Let's all go into the sitting room because the spices need to settle a little bit longer."

Jackie poured a glass of cognac and ginger ale for me and asked Jung Lee what she would like to have.

"I'll have the same as John." She poured champagne for herself and Mom. "You look so familiar, where do I know you from?"

"I work at the Manassas Airport. John and I used to chauffer executives around the country."

"Dad, are you ever going to take that long, extended vacation that you were talking about?"

"Yes, but I'm not going out of the country. I'm going to stay here. I'll do some cleaning up here and around my place, and I'll get more involved with The Jade Dragon."

"Are you going to retire from the business?"

"You've shown me that you're more than capable of handling the business yourself. If you need help, you know whom you can call on. I'll stay away for a while."

"The city already has a new Jack Delaplane to help fight crime."

•••

The End

9 798896 390183